Can you Dance to the Boogaloo?

Alice V. Lickens

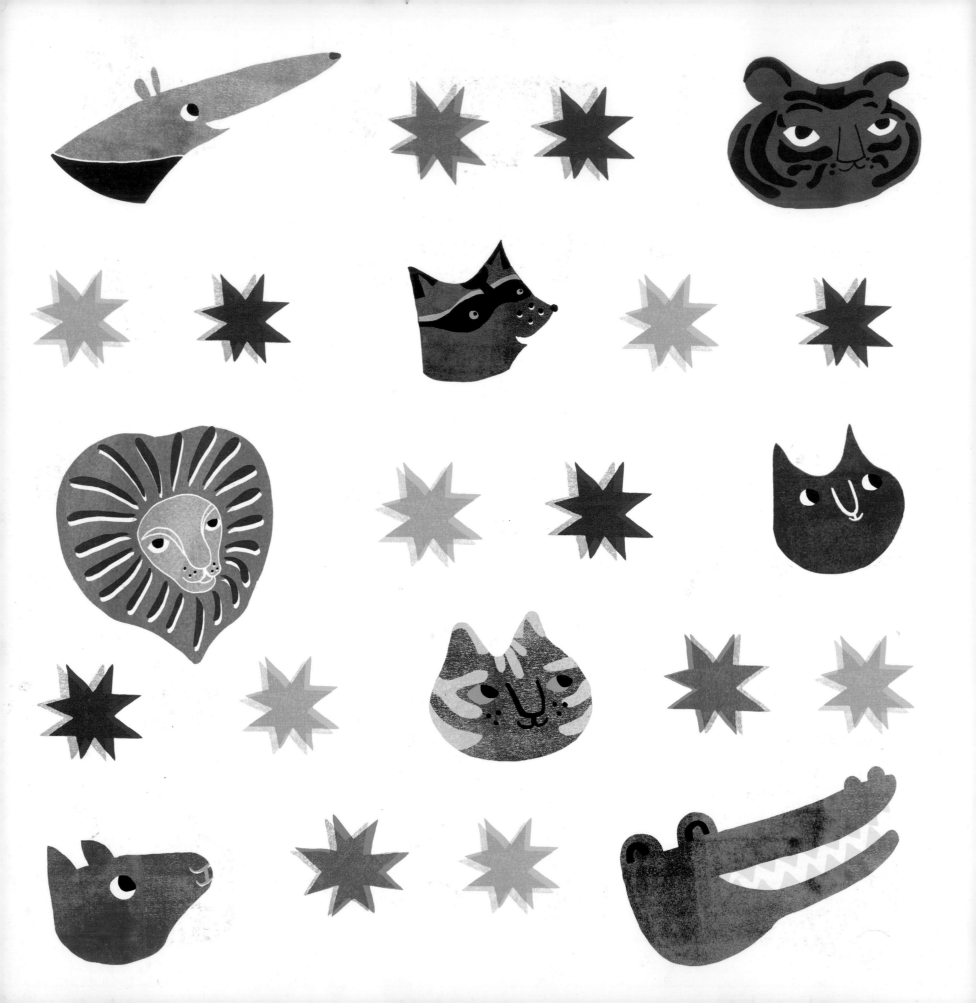

This book belongs to

....

This edition first published in the
United Kingdom in 2013
by Pavilion Children's Books,
10 Southcombe Street,
London, W14 0RA

Design and layout © Pavilion Children's Books 2013
Text and illustrations © Alice Lickens 2013

Associate Publisher: Ben Cameron
Designer: Claire Marshall
Commissioning Editor: Katie Deane
Production Controller: Helen Gerry

ISBN: 9781-84365-229-8

A CIP catalogue record for this book
is available from the British Library.

10 9 8 7 6 5 4 3 2 1

Reproduction by Mission, Hong Kong
Printed and bound in China.

This book can be ordered directly from the
publisher online at www.anovabooks.com

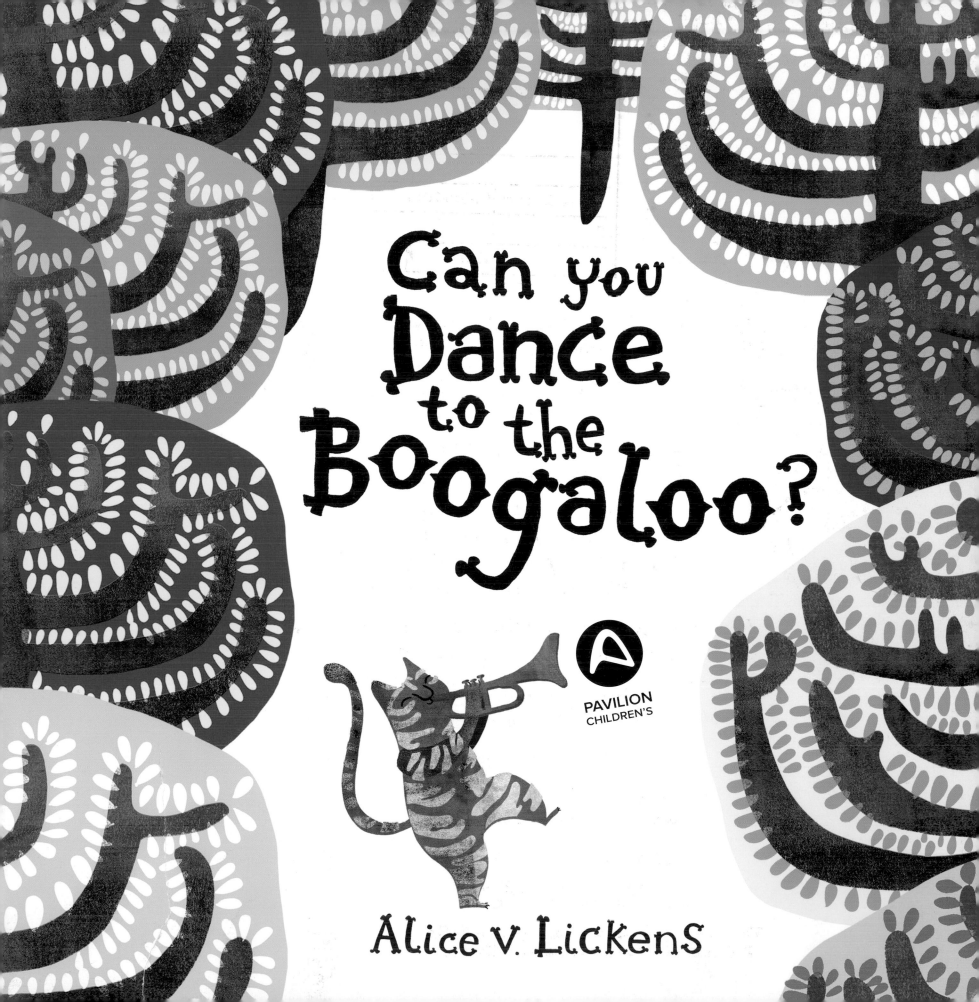

Can you Dance to the Boogaloo?

PAVILION
CHILDREN'S

Alice V. Lickens

When
there's a
beat
in your
Chest

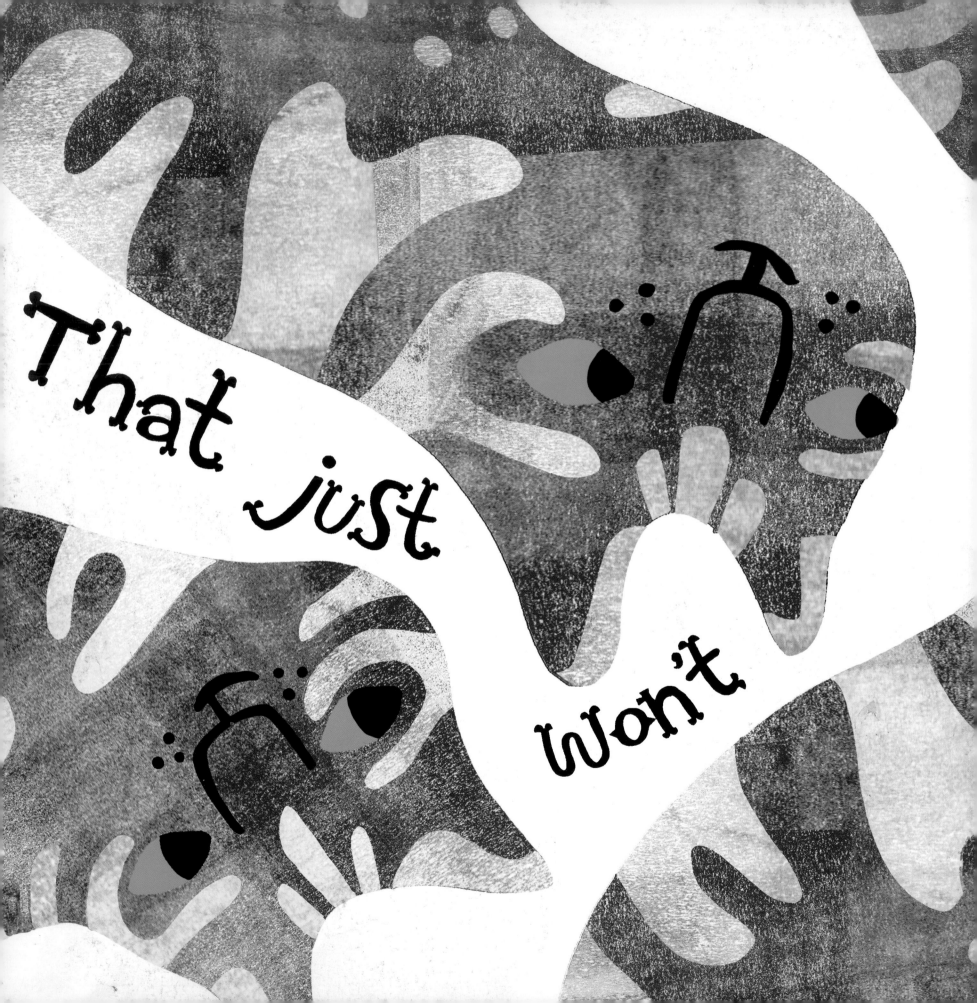

be put to rest

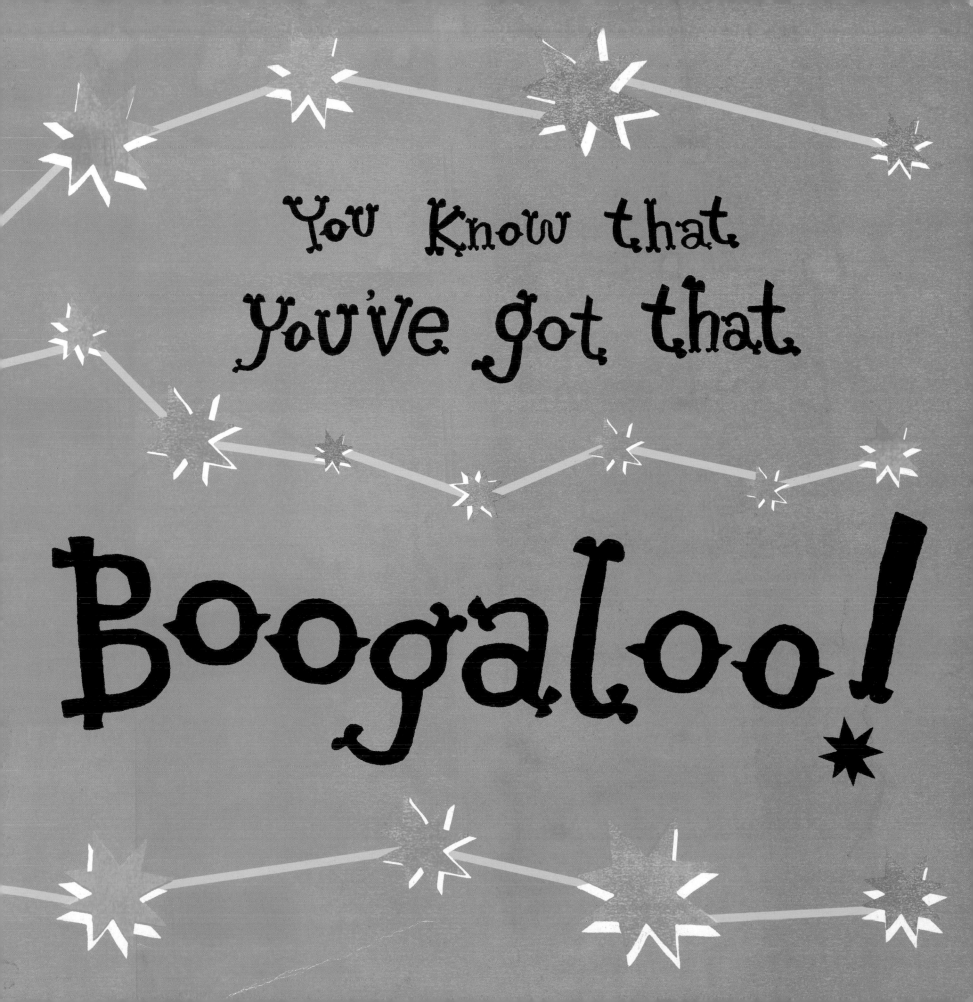

If there's a jump in

your feet and your

toes tap themselves

to the street

When your muscles begin to creep

and your
heart
starts to
RUMBLE

There's a hopity, honking blues

moving right
through your
bones

Come dance out of your den

Come jig and bop

Come roll those
toes to the hum

Hop till you can't Stop

jingle till you jangle

For my parents
Juliet & Howard,
who never fail
to amaze &
endure me